Th
Milk Van

by Nick Williams
illustrated by Steven Hallam

Harcourt
SCHOOL PUBLISHERS

Printed in the United States of America

ISBN 10: 0-15-351219-9
ISBN 13: 978-0-15-351219-3

Ordering Options
ISBN 10: 0-15-351211-3 (Grade 1 Advanced Collection)
ISBN 13: 978-0-15-351211-7 (Grade 1 Advanced Collection)
ISBN 10: 0-15-358016-X (package of 5)
ISBN 13: 978-0-15-358016-1 (package of 5)

2 3 4 5 6 7 8 9 10   179   15 14 13 12 11 10 09 08 07

My dad has a big van.

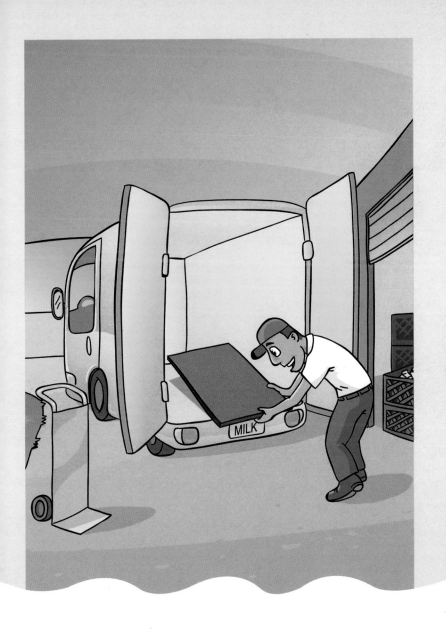

His van has a ramp.

Dad will get the milk.

Soon Dad will fill the van with milk.

The van can hold so much.

Soon Dad will come
home.

Dad will give me milk, too.